ANGRY

by Kerry Dinmont

The Child's World
childsworld.com

Published by The Child's World®
1980 Lookout Drive • Mankato, MN 56003-1705
800-599-READ • www.childsworld.com

Photographs ©: Shutterstock Images, cover, 1, 4, 8, 9, 10, 16, 17, 18, 22 (bottom left), 22 (bottom right); PR Image Factory/Shutterstock Images, 5, 6; Martin Novak/Shutterstock Images, 13; iStockphoto, 14; VG Stock Studio/Shutterstock Images, 21; Hans Kim/Shutterstock Images, 22 (top left); Anucha Pongpatimeth/Shutterstock Images, 22 (top right)

Design Elements: Shutterstock Images

ISBN Hardcover: 9781503828032
ISBN Paperback: 9781622434633
LCCN: 2018944225

Printed in the United States of America
PA02395

ABOUT THE AUTHOR

Kerry Dinmont is a children's book author who enjoys art and nature. She lives in Montana with her two Norwegian elkhounds.

CONTENTS

Chapter One

BELLE IS ANGRY

Belle loves playing video games.

She is playing a new game.

She is having a lot of fun.

Belle's mother comes to tell her dinner is ready. She tells Belle to stop her game. Belle shouts at her. Belle is angry.

Chapter Two

BEING ANGRY

Angry people have strong feelings toward someone or something. The angry person may be **annoyed**. He may feel **hurt**.

Many things can make people angry. Losing a spot in line can make someone angry. Some people get angry if someone else breaks their toys, too.

THINK ABOUT IT

What makes you angry?

Being angry might make you want to scream. You might want to hit someone or something. But these are not nice. Do not hurt other people. You can yell into a pillow instead.

It is okay to feel angry sometimes. Take a deep breath. Try to be **calm**. Drawing or listening to music might help. If someone hurt your feelings, calmly tell that person why it made you angry.

Chapter Three

BE KIND TO OTHERS

Your friends might get angry. They might say mean things. They might throw something. Do not get angry back.

Try not to be upset if someone is angry with you. You can give them some time alone.

If you hurt your friend, say you are sorry. Your friend might stay angry for a while. But an **apology** makes it easier to be friends again.

WHO IS ANGRY?

Can you tell who is angry? Turn to page 24 for the answer.

A

B

C

D

GLOSSARY

annoyed (uh-NOYD) Someone who is annoyed is upset and has lost patience with something. People might get angry because something has annoyed them.

apology (uh-PAH-luh-gee) An apology is when someone says he or she is sorry for something said or done. An apology makes it easier to stay friends with someone you made angry.

calm (KALM) To be calm is to feel relaxed and at peace. Coloring can help you feel calm.

hurt (HERT) To hurt someone is to make them feel bad physically or emotionally. You might get angry because someone hurt your feelings.

TO LEARN MORE

Books

Dinmont, Kerry. ***Dan's First Day of School: A Book about Emotions***. Mankato, MN: The Child's World, 2018.

Millar, Goldie. **F Is for Feelings**. Minneapolis, MN: Free Spirit Publishing, 2014.

Nilsen, Genevieve. **Angry**. Minneapolis, MN: Jump!, Inc., 2018.

Web Sites

Visit our Web site for links about anger:
childsworld.com/links

Note to Parents, Teachers, and Librarians: We routinely verify our Web links to make sure they are safe and active sites. So encourage your readers to check them out!

INDEX

Page 22
answer: **D**